DEXTER

DEXTER

By Clyde Robert Bulla

Illustrated by Glo Coalson

THOMAS Y. CROWELL COMPANY New York

Library of Congress Cataloging in Publication Data
Bulla, Clyde Robert.
 Dexter.
 SUMMARY: Dave befriends the strange new family and their pony,
Dexter, when the rest of the townspeople remain aloof.
 [1. Horses—Stories]   I. Coalson, Glo, illus.   II. Title.
PZ7.B912De   [Fic]   73–5595
  ISBN 0–690–00121–5   ISBN 0–690–00122–3 (lib. bdg.)

1 2 3 4 5 6 7 8 9 10

To Betty and Sid Fleischman

By the Author

Contents

The New People

One winter evening Dave's father came home from town and said, "We're going to have new neighbors."

Mother was putting supper on the table. She looked up quickly and asked, "Who?"

Dave had been reading, with his chair close to the kitchen stove. Now he put his book aside and listened.

Dave was twelve. He had always lived on the farm. The nearest city was a long way off. Even the town, where they sold cream and eggs and bought their groceries, was miles away. He didn't often see anyone new. In all his life he had never had new neighbors.

1

"I don't know who they are," said Father. "I just heard that somebody bought the old Temple place."

"The *Temple* place?" said Mother.

"That's what I heard," said Father, and they looked at each other, shaking their heads a little.

They all knew the Temple place wasn't much of a farm. No one had lived there for years. Most of the land had grown up in weeds and timber. The barn and sheds were beginning to fall apart. But the square, stone house had lasted a hundred years and might last a hundred more

Dave could hardly eat supper for thinking about the new people. He could hardly sleep that night for wondering about them.

He always walked past the Temple place on his way to school. The next morning he stopped for a look at the old house. It was tall and gray, with two chimneys that stood out against the sky. It was set far back off the road at the end of a lane. With snow on the roof and the front windows broken, it looked cold and lonesome.

Wayne Ogle came out into the road. He was Dave's age, and he lived just across from the Temple place.

"Did you hear about the new people?" asked Dave.

"What new people?" asked Wayne.

"They're going to live on the old Temple place," said Dave.

"Who?" asked Wayne. "Mr. and Mrs. Spider? Mr. and Mrs. Rat?"

Dave told him what Father had said.

"Nobody would live there," said Wayne.

"Somebody might," said Dave.

"I'll believe it when I see it," said Wayne.

They went on to school. The schoolhouse was in a yard between two cornfields. Boys and girls were playing fox-and-geese in the snow while they waited for the bell to ring.

"Did you hear about the new neighbors?" asked Dave.

None of them had. They stopped playing and crowded about him on the schoolhouse steps.

Mrs. Howard, the teacher, opened the door and looked out. "What's this—what's this?" she asked.

"People are going to live on the Temple place," Dave told her.

"Will there be any children?" asked Mary Haines, one of the older girls.

"There might be," said Dave.

"They might be in school," said Mary.

"If they're over six and under fourteen, they certainly will," said Mrs. Howard. "It's the law."

Wayne Ogle kept saying, "Nobody's going to live on that old place," but no one wanted to listen to him.

"Where do you think the new people will come from?" asked Mary.

"Maybe a long way," said Dave, "like New York."

"Or California," said Mary. "How many will be in the family, do you think?"

4

Little Gracie Cooper spoke up. "I think they'll have three girls and one boy and a dog, too!"

Dave didn't say so, but he hoped there would be a boy his age. He hoped the boy would like to skate and swim and maybe read books and talk about them.

On his way home from school he stopped for another look at the old stone house. There was still an hour before sundown. He waded through snow to the front door and went inside. The big rooms were chilly and bare. Glass and dirt crunched under his feet.

He had been in the house before, but now he was seeing it in a different way. He was seeing it as it might look to someone coming here to live. Water had left purple stains on the walls and ceilings. A step in the stairs was broken. Wasps had built their mud nests across the fireplace.

He looked at the rooms, upstairs and down. Then he went home.

"Where have you been?" asked Mother.

"In the old house," answered Dave. "It looks pretty bad. Do you think we could fix it up a little before the people come?"

"No, I don't," she said.

"I could do it myself," said Dave. "I could take a broom and—"

"It's their house, not ours," said Mother. "They might not want us going into it."

"Your mother is right," said Father.

The winter days grew longer. Dave began to smell spring in the air.

Whenever he went past the old stone house, he looked for the new neighbors. Wayne Ogle laughed at him for looking. "Nobody's going to live there," he said. "My father says so."

One Monday morning Dave was running to school. He was late because he had helped Father drive the cows to pasture. The March wind pushed him along.

He almost went past the Temple place without looking, but from habit he did look. He stopped. There was a truck in front of the house. Out by the road was a post with a new mailbox on it.

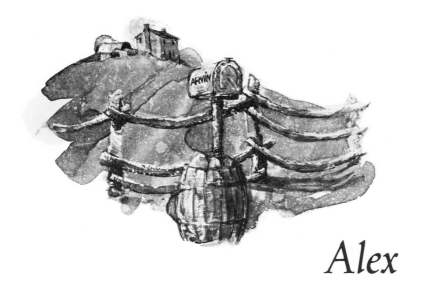

Alex

The name on the mailbox was "Arvin." No one at school had ever heard it before. The boys and girls said it over and over, "Arvin—Arvin."

"It may be a foreign name," said the teacher.

"Do you think they're foreign people?" asked Mary Haines.

"They look like it to me," said Wayne Ogle. He felt important because he was the only one who had seen them. "There are two men and a woman and a boy. The men have mustaches—black mustaches—and they wear boots. They all talk a lot, but they're across the road, so I can't hear what they say."

"I wonder if the boy will be in school," said the teacher.

"He looks too old," said Wayne.

Later they heard that the boy *was* too old. He was fifteen.

They found out more about the Arvins. The boy's name was Alex. His mother and father were Yetty and Paul. The other man was Jon, Paul's older brother. They had two cows, a team of horses, and three pigs, and the boy had a pony.

Dave saw the people as he went by. He saw them working about the house and barn. Then school was out, and he had no good reason to go by anymore.

But he kept hearing new things about the Arvins. They worked hard, although they didn't know much about farming. They were putting a fence around the land when they should have been plowing and planting.

Dave's mother talked about going to see Mrs. Arvin. "But I don't know whether to go or not," she said. "I hear such odd things."

One of the things was that Yetty Arvin wore strange-looking clothes. And the Ogles said the new people weren't friendly.

"I'm never going there again," said Wayne. He told Dave what had happened. He had gone to see the pony, and he had asked Alex a few questions—"Where did you get your pony?" "How much did he cost?" "Where did you come from?" "How did you happen to buy this farm?" "What did you do before you came here?"

Alex hadn't answered any of them. All he had said was, "You want to know quite a lot, don't you?"

"He thinks he's something big because he's got that pony," said Wayne. "It's not so much. It's *funny*-looking. It's got orange-colored spots."

Dave told his mother, "I'd like to see the pony up close. I'm going over there."

"I don't think they want to see any of us," she said.

"I'll just walk by," he said, "and maybe the pony will be out in the pasture."

It was a Sunday afternoon. Dave walked past Arvins'. He saw no one, and the pony was nowhere in sight.

The day was warm. He stopped to rest before he started home.

While he stood in the road, he heard the pounding of hoofs. Over the hill came Alex Arvin on his pony. The pony's mane and tail were flying. Alex was leaning forward in the saddle like a trick rider. They came up so suddenly that Dave had to jump to get out of the way. He fell backward into the ditch.

He picked himself up. Alex had stopped and was riding back.

Dave felt foolish, but Alex was not laughing.

"Are you all right?" he asked.

"I think so," said Dave.

"There's blood on your hand," said Alex.

Dave looked at his hand. "I must have scratched it."

"We'd better take care of it. Come on up to the house." Alex jumped down. He led the pony and walked beside Dave.

"I guess you know I'm Alex Arvin," he said.

"I'm Dave Weber," said Dave.

"And this is Dexter." Alex patted the pony's neck. The pony was dancing along as if he would rather run than walk. Once he put his head down and took a nip at Alex's arm.

"He bit you!" said Dave.

Alex laughed. "He was pretending. He likes to pretend he's a wild horse."

Dave had been looking at Dexter. The pony's spots were not orange-colored. They were a dark red-brown. "I never saw a horse like him before," he said.

"He's part Indian pony," said Alex. "We've been together a long time now. My father and I went to this place where the horses were, and Dexter and I chose each other."

"How do you mean?" asked Dave.

"I went straight to him, and he came straight to me. People said his legs were too short and he was too thick through the chest. It didn't matter to me. Dexter was my horse, and that was all I cared about."

They went up to the house. Alex's mother was in the doorway. She looked like a girl. Her black hair hung to her shoulders. She wore a long, flowered dress, and she was barefoot.

"This is Dave," said Alex. "He hurt his hand."

"It isn't anything," said Dave, but she led him inside, brought a washcloth, and washed his hand.

"It isn't a deep scratch," she said. "I don't think we need to wrap it up."

Dave looked about the front room. There was new glass where the broken windowpanes had been. The floor was clean. But the walls were still cracked and spotted, and there was hardly any furniture in the room.

The two men came in. They had long, dark faces like Alex's. The younger man said, "I'm Alex's father. I'm Paul Arvin," and he shook Dave's hand. The other man said nothing, but he made a little bow. There was something mocking about it.

"Sit down, everyone," said Mrs. Arvin. "It's teatime."

They sat on the floor at a low table. The table was two boards with bricks for legs. In the middle was a glass jar with yellow weed-flowers in it.

Mrs. Arvin brought tea and cakes. The cakes had an odd taste, but Dave liked them. They were made with spices that he had never tasted before. She kept passing them to him, but he ate only two. Then he said he had to go.

"I'll give you a ride home," said Alex.

"Oh, I can walk," said Dave.

"Dexter needs the exercise," said Alex.

Dave saw that Alex wanted to take him home. "All right," he said.

As they all got up from the table, Alex's uncle asked Dave, "What brought you here?"

Dave didn't understand.

"No other neighbor has set foot in this house since we've

been here," said Alex's uncle. "They've come to the fence to ask questions, but they've never been to the house. What brought you?"

Alex spoke. "I asked him."

"I see," said his uncle. He looked down at Dave, and again he made his mocking little bow.

The Barn Loft

Dave waited a day. Then he said, "I'm going over to Arvins'."

"I thought you didn't like Alex's Uncle Jon," said Mother.

"I'm going to see Alex and Dexter," said Dave.

"Are you sure Alex wants to see you?" asked Mother. "He's so much older than you are."

Father told Dave, "That boy has work to do, and so have you."

So Dave stayed at home and hoed the potatoes.

The next day there was rain, and the garden was too wet to hoe.

"I'm going to Arvins'," said Dave.

"That boy took you home with him because you hurt your hand," said Mother. "That doesn't mean he wants you to come back."

"No," said Dave, "but I think he does."

He put on his overshoes and raincoat and went out. The rain had stopped, but more was on the way. Clouds were black across the west.

He turned in at Arvins'. Mrs. Arvin came to the door. "I don't know where Alex is," she said. "He may be in the barn."

Dave went to the barn. As he stepped inside, the rain began to pour.

The barn felt dry. The Arvins must have put on a new roof, he thought. There was hay in the loft. He could see bunches of it hanging through the square opening over his head.

The cows and workhorses were in the stalls on one side of the barn. In the big box stall on the other side was Dexter. The pony watched him, rolling his eyes a little.

Dave laughed at him. "Wild horse!" he said.

He called up into the loft, "Alex? Hello!" The sound of the rain drowned out his voice.

A ladder led to the loft. He climbed it. He stopped with his head through the opening, not quite believing what he saw.

Three trapezes hung in a row from the roof. On the first one stood Alex—Alex in black tights with silver spangles! He was standing with one knee bent and one arm out.

Suddenly he dropped off the trapeze and caught it in both

hands. He swung and caught the next one. He swung to the third trapeze and caught it.

For a minute or two he seemed to be flying back and forth across the barn. Again he stood up on the first trapeze. He leaped for the next one. He saw Dave's face below. He lost his hold and fell.

Dave came on up the ladder. "Alex!" he said. "Did it hurt you?"

Alex was lying on the hay. He didn't look at Dave. "No," he said. "It didn't hurt me."

"Did I make you fall?" asked Dave.

Alex got up and disappeared behind a pile of hay. When he came out he had on a shirt and overalls.

Dave said, "What you were doing up there—that was *good!*"

Alex climbed down the ladder. Dave followed him into the stall where Dexter was. The pony snorted and shied away.

"Is he afraid of me?" asked Dave.

"No," said Alex. He took a brush down from a nail and began to brush the pony.

Dave wanted to ask about the trapezes, but there was something in Alex's face that stopped him. Alex looked almost angry as he brushed away at Dexter's coat.

Dave went to the door. The rain was stopping. "I'd better go," he said.

He waited outside, giving Alex a chance to call him back, but Alex didn't call.

Dave went home. His mother said, "You didn't stay long."

"Alex was busy," he said.

The next day was too wet for Dave to work outside. In his room he tried to read, but he didn't feel like reading. He kept thinking about what he had seen in Arvins' barn. Alex flying across the loft like a bird. Alex looking as if he were angry. Had he been angry because Dave had seen him on the trapezes?

If I could do those things, I wouldn't keep it a secret, Dave thought. I'd *want* everyone to see me.

Or maybe Alex had been angry because Dave had made him fall. Yet he'd fallen on the hay. He couldn't have been hurt.

Dave put down his book and picked it up again. The gate clicked open and shut, and he looked out. A pony was tied in front of the house. It was Dexter!

He ran to the door. Alex was on the porch.

"Are you doing anything?" he asked.

"No," said Dave.

"Do you want to come over to my house?" asked Alex.

The Family Secret

The road was muddy. When they got to Arvins', Dexter's legs and sides were splashed. Alex took him into the barn and sponged him off. All the time he talked to the pony—"That was a good ride. Did you like it? Maybe I don't ride you enough. Uncle Jon says you're getting too fat. Now what do you think of that?"

Dave must have looked puzzled, because Alex asked him, "Don't you talk to your horses?"

"Not much," answered Dave. "Just 'whoa' and 'get up.'"

"Dexter likes for me to talk to him," said Alex.

Dexter pawed the dirt floor.

"Now he's talking to me," said Alex. "He's saying, 'I want out.'" He turned the pony out into the pasture. They watched him trot off toward the timber. Then Alex led the way up into the loft.

They sat on the hay under the trapezes.

Alex said, "I thought you wouldn't come over today."

"Why not?" asked Dave.

"I wasn't very friendly yesterday."

"Oh," said Dave.

"I shouldn't have blamed you, just because you found out the family secret," said Alex. "I was being pretty stupid."

Dave looked at him, trying to understand what he was saying.

"I didn't care, for myself," said Alex. "There's nothing wrong with being in the circus. But my father and Uncle Jon thought it was better not to tell because—"

"The circus!" said Dave. "You were in the circus?"

Alex gave him a long look. "You mean you didn't guess?"

Dave shook his head.

"Where did you think I learned the trapezes?" asked Alex. "Where did you think I got the tights I was wearing?"

"I didn't think about that," said Dave.

"You *would* have thought about it after a while," said Alex. "And the people you told—*they'd* have thought about it."

"I didn't tell anyone," said Dave.

"You didn't? Not even your mother and father?"

"No," said Dave.

"You didn't tell *anyone*?"

"No."

"Why not?"

"The way you acted," said Dave, "I thought it was a secret."

"And if I told you a secret, you wouldn't tell anybody?"

"Not if you didn't want me to," said Dave.

They were quiet for a while.

Alex asked, "Did you ever wonder why we bought this place and came here?"

"Yes," said Dave.

"Do you want me to tell you why?"

"Not if you don't want to."

"I want to. I think we're going to be friends, and if we're friends we have to trust each other." They were all circus people, Alex said, he and his mother and father and Uncle Jon. Even Dexter was a circus horse. "My father and Uncle Jon had a trapeze act, and they were teaching me. My mother rode horses in the ring, but she never liked the circus much.

"About two years ago Uncle Jon had his fall. He fell off a high trapeze. The net caught him. He wasn't hurt. But he wasn't the same after that. He had headaches and dizzy spells. My father didn't feel safe working with him anymore.

"Last summer we were on our way from Texas to Chicago. We were driving our own truck and seeing the country. We got lost and came past this place. My mother saw the house, and she said it was what she'd wanted all her life. We talked

22

about coming here and being farmers. It was just in fun at first, then my mother said she really meant it. My father wanted to make her happy. Uncle Jon said he'd always wanted to be a farmer."

"What about you?" asked Dave.

"I like the circus," said Alex, "but I thought I might like the country, too. We put in all the money we had. It wasn't enough, but Uncle Jon sold the house he had and came here and bought the farm. When we moved in, we wanted to be like everybody else here. We were afraid the neighbors would think we were odd if they knew we were circus people, so we didn't tell anybody. It wouldn't have mattered, I guess. They think we're odd anyway. They think we were crazy to buy this place. They laugh at the way we run the farm."

"You've done a lot of work here," said Dave.

"Yes, but we don't seem to grow anything." Alex picked up a handful of hay. "We had to buy this. It's mostly for Dexter. Uncle Jon said the pony could eat grass, but Dexter likes hay, too, and he's used to it."

"Besides, it makes a good landing place under the trapezes," said Dave.

"Yes, it does. Do you want to try them?" asked Alex.

"I couldn't even get up there," said Dave.

"It's easy. See? I nailed those pieces of wood up the wall. You can climb them like a ladder. Then you reach out and catch the first trapeze. Try it."

Dave tried it. He caught the trapeze. His hands slipped off

23

and he fell. He bounced on the hay and lay there, getting his breath.

"That wasn't bad. You made a good fall," said Alex. "Maybe we can work up an act together—after you've practiced a few weeks."

"A few years, you mean." But Dave was excited, thinking how it might be—he and Alex in the top of a circus tent. He and Alex on trapezes, with a thousand faces looking up from below.

Alex's Hideaway

When Dave went home, he found a place to practice. It was in a cherry tree behind the house. Some of the branches grew out almost straight from the trunk. He practiced swinging on them.

The next Sunday he went to Arvins'. Alex came to the gate to meet him.

"I've been practicing," said Dave.

"Practicing?" said Alex.

"You know—for our great circus act." Dave made a joke of it, but Alex didn't smile.

They went to the barn. Without a word, Alex led the way up the ladder.

Dave looked into the loft. The trapezes were gone!

The ropes had been cut. Only the short ends were left.

"What—?" he began.

"Uncle Jon did it," said Alex. "I came out yesterday, and he had the ladder up and was sawing away with his knife."

"Why?" asked Dave.

"He said I spent too much time out here. He said we should all work harder. Then we'd be better farmers, and everyone wouldn't be laughing at us." Alex's face was bitter. "If he didn't want me to have the trapezes, why didn't he *say* so? I'd have taken them down. He didn't have to . . . well, it's done, and that's the end of it. Come on. Let's get out of here."

They went outside.

"After Uncle Jon cut the ropes, I went to the timber," said Alex. "I stayed all day, and I found something. I'll show you."

They walked across the pasture and into the timber. The trees grew close together. Only a little sunlight came through.

They came to the creek. The water was dark and deep. They walked across on a fallen tree.

"There's what I found," said Alex, "between those two pine trees."

It was the four walls of an old log cabin almost covered by a mat of vines.

"I remember this!" said Dave. "Wayne Ogle and I saw it a long time ago. Father said it was here when he was a boy. He didn't know who built it or why."

"There's a door somewhere," said Alex.

Dave was poking with a stick. "Here it is. Father said the cabin was never finished," Dave went on. "He didn't think it ever had a roof."

"Let's give it one," said Alex.

"A flat roof would be easy," said Dave. "We could lay poles across the top and cover them with sod. That's how people made roofs a long time ago."

"Maybe I'll put in a floor, too," said Alex, "and put up a sign that says 'Alex's Hideaway.' Maybe I'll live here and be a hermit!"

He laughed, but Dave had a feeling he was half-serious.

Several times that summer Alex talked of finishing the cabin.

"I'll help," said Dave.

"All right. It will be your cabin, too," said Alex. "Let's see if we can get it done before cold weather."

Summer had seemed so long. Then, all at once, it was over. School had begun, and the cabin was just as Alex had found it.

In October the school planned a Halloween party. "It will be for us and our families," said Mrs. Howard.

"And friends?" asked Mary Haines.

"Yes, our friends, too."

"What about the Arvins?" asked Dave.

For a few moments the schoolroom was quiet.

"I don't know—" began Mrs. Howard.

"They might get into a fight," said Wayne Ogle. "The two men are always fighting. I can hear them all the way to my house."

"We don't want any fights, do we?" said the teacher. "I suppose we'd better not ask them."

"If we ask everyone else, won't they feel left out?" asked Dave.

"I don't think so," said Mrs. Howard. "I really don't think they'd want to come."

A few days before the party Mrs. Howard asked the boys and girls to bring pumpkins to school. "For jack-o'-lanterns," she said. "We'll decorate the schoolroom with them."

That evening Dave went to the garden and chose a pumpkin. It was round and coppery-gold. When he brought it to the house, Mother said, "It's so big. How will you get it to school?"

"I know how," he said.

In the morning he started to school, carrying the pumpkin on his head. It *was* a big pumpkin. He thought what a good jack-o'-lantern it would make.

He came to Arvins'. The farm looked bare. There was something sad about the thin curl of smoke that came from the chimney.

Almost without thinking, he turned in at the gate. He saw no one as he walked up to the house. He put the pumpkin down in front of the door and left it there.

"Take Care of Dexter"

Winter came, and Dave saw Alex less and less. It was too cold for them to stay long in the barn or the timber. Dave felt strange about going to Alex's house, and Alex seemed to feel strange about coming to Dave's.

One day after school they met at Arvins' gate. As they talked, they stamped their feet to keep warm.

"Things are getting worse," said Alex.

"What things?" asked Dave.

"Things at home. It's Uncle Jon. He's been saying we're all against him. Now he says we have to go."

"Go where?" asked Dave.

"He doesn't care, as long as we're out of his way."

"He couldn't make you go," said Dave. "It's three against one."

"He says the farm was bought in his name. He says he can put us out anytime he wants to."

"Do you think he can?" asked Dave.

"Maybe. I don't know. My father says he won't go. He says he's put too much time and money into this place to walk out and leave it."

"Your uncle couldn't farm it by himself," said Dave.

"He doesn't think about that." The wind blew snow into Alex's face, and he shivered. "Well—sometimes there's nothing you can do but wait. Dave, I have to go in. I have to chop some wood, or there won't be any supper."

Dave asked him, "How is Dexter?"

"Dexter?" Alex grinned suddenly. "He's all right. I haven't told him there's anything wrong!"

Dave got a sled for Christmas. It was the biggest and best one he had ever had. He told Alex, "Come over, and we'll go coasting."

But weeks went by, and Alex never came. Then the snow was gone, and it was too late.

The last day of school there was a picnic in the schoolyard. Afterward Dave stopped to see Alex. They talked out by the gate.

"Let's go over to the cabin some day," said Alex.

"Alex's Hideaway?" said Dave.

"Alex and Dave's Hideaway. I worked on it yesterday."

"What did you do?"

"Cleared away some of the brush. I'll show you when you come over. What are you doing Sunday?"

"I'll see," said Dave.

The next day was Saturday. It was a stormy day, with wind and rain. That night there was a thunderstorm that shook the house, but in the morning the sun was shining across Dave's bed. He thought, I can go to Alex's.

Breakfast was late.

"With all the thunder and lightning, I couldn't get to sleep till nearly morning," said Mother. "Then I overslept."

They were still at the table when footsteps came up across the porch. Father went to the door. Mr. Ogle and Wayne were outside.

They clumped into the kitchen in their rubber boots. Their eyes were bright and their faces were red. They began to talk at once, in loud, hoarse voices.

"Slow down," said Father. "I can't hear what you're saying."

"I said, I couldn't call you on the telephone," said Mr. Ogle. "The telephone line's not working. The wind blew down some poles. Yes, sir, it was quite a night."

"Yes, we had a bad storm," said Father.

"I didn't mean the storm," said Mr. Ogle. "You don't know the things that happened last night."

"Jon Arvin—" began Wayne.

33

His father gave him a shake. "You just keep quiet. *I'm* telling this."

Dave had stopped eating. He asked, "What about Jon Arvin?"

"The sheriff came out," said Wayne, "and he—"

"I told you to keep quiet." His father gave him another shake. "You weren't there, and I was, and I'm telling this."

He went on with his story. He told it slowly, as if he enjoyed it and wanted to make it last.

Yesterday afternoon the sheriff and his son had come out to Arvins'. They were on horseback, because the roads were too muddy for a car. Mr. Ogle went over to see what was happening. He found out that Jon Arvin wanted to put the rest of the Arvins off the place. Jon had seen a lawyer, and the lawyer had gone to the sheriff. Jon was waiting in town till the sheriff had put the others off the farm.

But Paul Arvin wouldn't go. He had locked himself in the house with his wife and son.

It got dark, and the storm got worse. The sheriff and his son took their horses to the barn and put them in the box stall with Dexter, where it was dry.

The sheriff hadn't brought a flashlight, so Mr. Ogle went home and got one. The sheriff flashed the light on the house and said, "I didn't come here to make trouble, but if you don't come out, there's going to *be* trouble."

No one answered. The sheriff and his son fired their guns over the roof.

"Open the door," said the sheriff, "unless you want me to shoot the lock off. And if I do that, somebody might get hurt."

Paul Arvin called out, "Don't shoot anymore. I have my wife and son here." He opened the door. "Here I am," he said. "Come on and arrest me."

The sheriff said, "I told you I didn't want trouble. All I'm supposed to do is see that you get off this farm."

"Now?" asked Paul Arvin. "In the middle of the night?"

"It wasn't the middle of the night when I first told you to come out," said the sheriff. Still, he seemed to feel sorry for them. He asked Mr. Ogle if he would hitch up a team of horses and take the Arvins to town. "I'll see that they find a place to stay," the sheriff said, "and you'll be paid for your trouble."

Mr. Ogle brought over a team and wagon. The Arvins were waiting. "I'll ride Dexter," said Alex.

They went to the barn. They flashed the light into the box stall, and then they saw the terrible thing that had happened. Crowded together in the dark, the sheriff's horses and Dexter had fought. Dexter was lying on the floor of the stall. He was lying very still, with his head twisted to one side.

"Keep the boy away," said the sheriff. "Don't let him see."

Alex was already in the stall. He was holding Dexter's head. "Get a doctor," he said. "We've got to get a doctor!"

His father ran his hands over Dexter's chest and neck. "It's too late," he said. "He's gone. Can't you see?"

He dragged Alex away.

36

The flashlight flickered and burned out. They all felt their way back to the wagon. The sheriff tried to tell the Arvins he was sorry. Paul Arvin wouldn't talk to him. Mrs. Arvin was crying. Alex was saying, "I won't go!" But when the others got into the wagon, he got in, too.

Mr. Ogle drove them to town. The sheriff found them a place to stay, but they wouldn't take it.

As Mr. Ogle came to the end of his story, Dave got up from the table. "Where are they?" he asked. "*Where did they go?*"

"To the railroad station," said Mr. Ogle. "They were going to wait for the train. The boy wanted me to tell you something. He said, 'Tell Dave to take care of Dexter.' "

"Keep Out"

Mr. Ogle and Wayne were gone. Dave heard the door close after them.

Father was talking. His voice sounded a long way off. Dave went to the corner where the overshoes and rubber boots were kept. He began to put on his overshoes.

"Where are you going?" asked Mother.

"To town," he said.

"You can't *walk* to town."

"Yes, I can," he said, "and I'll bring Alex back with me— so he'll have a place to stay."

"Alex is with his father and mother," she said. "He wouldn't leave them."

"They can come, too," said Dave. "They can have my room."

"You can't help them this way," said Father. "They have plans of their own."

"You don't want them here!" said Dave. "You never did."

"Dave, listen," said Mother. "Maybe the Arvins aren't even in town. I'll call someone and try to find out." She went to the telephone. He heard her say, "It's still not working."

He had one overshoe on. He began to put on the other one.

"You are *not* going to town," said Father. "Long before you could get there, the telephone line will be fixed. Men are working on it now."

Slowly Dave put down the overshoe. He sat there, waiting.

Mother kept trying the telephone. Toward noon she said, "It's working again."

She called the railroad station and talked with someone. She told Dave, "The Arvins have gone. They left on the early train."

"Where did they go?" he asked.

"The man didn't know. It was the train that goes south."

"They had a home before they came here," said Father. "Maybe they've gone back to it."

Dave went to the door.

"Where are you going?" asked Mother.

"To take care of Dexter," he said.

"But the pony is—" She stopped. "Didn't you hear what Mr. Ogle said?"

"I heard him," said Dave. "Alex wanted me to bury his pony."

"How do you know?" asked Father.

"He asked me to take care of Dexter," said Dave. "What else could he have meant?"

He went outside. Father followed him. "I'll go with you."

"No," said Dave. "He wanted me to do it."

"You'll need help," said Father.

They took two shovels out of the woodshed. They walked to the Arvin place. The gate was wired shut.

Father started to climb over.

"There's someone here," said Dave.

A man stood in the doorway of the house. It was Jon Arvin.

He came out into the sunlight, walking slowly. Once he stumbled and almost fell. A little way from the gate he stopped and looked at them. His face was gray.

"Ah, the young gentleman. And the father," he said. "You wished to see me?"

"We didn't know anyone was here," said Father.

"Then why did you come?" asked Jon Arvin.

"There's something my boy and I wanted to take care of," said Father.

"All has been taken care of," said Jon Arvin. "I had no need of you before, and I have no need of you now." Then he shouted, "*Get out!*" and he began to cough.

40

Dave and his father drew back. Father said, as they turned toward home, "Jon Arvin is a sick man."

Two days later the Ogles had more news to tell. Mr. Norwood, Jon Arvin's lawyer, had come out from town with papers to be signed. No one had answered his knock. He had gone into the house and found Jon Arvin lying on the floor.

"It was a stroke," said Mr. Ogle. "He can't talk, and he doesn't know anybody. The lawyer had him moved to a hospital."

The next day a truck came and hauled away the two horses, the cows, the pigs, and the chickens. Someone nailed a "Keep Out" sign to the gate. Mr. Ogle said it was the lawyer.

The Face in the Bushes

Now there was more to the story of the Arvins.

"Jon Arvin got the place, but what good did it do him?" someone said. "He may never walk or talk again. That lawyer will get the whole farm someday."

"Yes, if he wants it," said someone else. "It's never been much good to anyone."

People knew Dave had been Alex's friend. They asked him questions—"What caused the trouble?" "Who started it?" "Where did Paul Arvin take his family?"

"I don't know—I don't know," he kept saying. What he wanted to say was, "Leave me alone!"

Wayne Ogle stopped by. He came into the barn lot, where Dave was pumping water for the cows.

"Did you ever hear from your friend?" he asked.

"What friend?" asked Dave.

"You know. Alex Arvin."

"No," said Dave.

"It's been a week. I guess you're not going to hear."

Dave waited for him to go, but Wayne sat down on the edge of the water tank.

"I know something I'm not supposed to tell."

"Then don't tell it," said Dave.

"I'll just tell you," said Wayne. "Who do you think was at the Arvin place yesterday?"

"The lawyer," said Dave.

"Somebody else. You'd never guess who. It was Mary."

"Mary Haines?"

"Yes. Mary Haines. She was hunting mushrooms—she and her cousin. They came running out of the timber like scared rabbits. Mary tore her dress getting over the fence."

"What were they running for?"

"They were close to that old cabin, and they thought they saw a ghost or something," said Wayne. "Mary said it looked like a bear, and her cousin thought it was a man. I was across the road when they came out of the timber. They didn't want me to tell. They weren't supposed to be there, you know."

"What do you think they saw?" asked Dave.

"I don't think they saw anything. Maybe they heard some

little sound, and they both started running. Mary always was scared of her shadow."

It wasn't true, Dave thought afterward. Mary *wasn't* scared of her shadow. In all the years they had gone to school together, he couldn't remember anything she *had* been scared of.

She saw something in the timber, he told himself. Mary saw *something*. . . .

That night he had a dream. He dreamed he was walking with Alex. Alex was talking. Dave tried to hear, but there was a wind that blew the words away.

He woke up. The dream still seemed real. For a few moments he thought Alex was in the room.

He lay there thinking. What if Alex had come back?

Once he had told Dave that he would live in the cabin and be a hermit. What if it had been Alex the girls had seen?

When it was daylight, Dave put on his clothes and went outside. The air was cool. The morning was still.

He cut across the fields to the Arvin timber. He pushed through bushes and vines to the cabin. Weeds and brush had been cleared from in front of the doorway. Poles had been cut and laid across the top of the cabin.

Alex had done the work. He knew it had been Alex!

He went into the cabin. It was an empty shell.

Now he remembered what Alex had said the last time they talked together—that he had worked on the cabin and cleared away some of the brush.

So Alex *had* done the work, but he had done it more than a week ago.

Dave began to feel foolish. Why had he thought Alex would be here? Mary Haines and her cousin had been frightened by something near the cabin. And Alex had once talked about living here and calling it his hideaway. Those were the only reasons.

Why *should* Alex have come back? What was there to bring him back?

Dave sat down on the leaves that covered the cabin floor. The sun was up. Mother would have breakfast ready. She would be calling him.

He knew he should be getting home. But he felt tired, and the leaves were like a bed. He leaned back. His eyes closed.

Then he was sitting up, his eyes open. He heard footsteps, strange and heavy and slow.

Through the doorway he saw the bushes moving. They parted, and a face looked out. It looked toward the cabin and disappeared.

It was a while before Dave could move again, before he could think. He got to his feet and went outside. He could still hear the slow, heavy steps. He began to run, following them. He fought his way through the bushes until he could see the moving figure ahead.

"Dexter!" he shouted. "*Dexter!*"

The horse stopped and looked back. Then he went plunging on, his hind legs dragging stiffly.

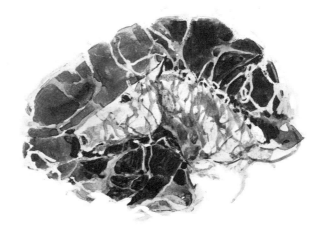

A Letter

Dave ran home. He said, "I saw Dexter. He's alive!"

Mother and Father were at the breakfast table. Mother was drinking coffee. Father was eating pancakes.

"Didn't you hear me?" Dave almost shouted it. "Alex's pony is alive!"

"Dave, why do you worry us this way?" asked Mother. "I went to your room, and you weren't there, and I—"

"That doesn't *matter!*" said Dave. "I just saw—"

"I think it does matter," said Father. "Why did you get up and go away without letting us know? Sit down and tell us what this is all about."

48

Dave sat down. He tried to speak slowly so they would understand. "I heard about someone—some people going into Arvins' timber. They thought they saw a ghost. I woke up early, and I was thinking about it, so I went over there, and *Dexter* came up. He was all scratched and crippled. . . ."

Now they were listening. They were beginning to believe him.

". . . The pony was always wild with everybody but Alex. He tried to run away from me. I was afraid he might hurt himself, so I didn't go too close—"

Mother said, "I don't see—I just don't see how it could have happened."

"I see how it *might* have happened," said Father. "Everybody *thought* the pony was dead, but no one made *sure*. It was night. There wasn't much light, and everybody was upset—"

"And after everybody was gone, Dexter dragged himself into the timber," said Dave. "That's how it happened. That's how it *has* to have happened." He asked, "Can we call Doc Gilman?"

"Doc Gilman is too old to go out on calls anymore," said Father.

"We could bring him out," said Dave.

"Yes," said Father. "Yes, I suppose we could."

They were nearly to town when Father remembered something. "The farm is Jon Arvin's, and the lawyer put up a

49

'Keep Out' sign. We'll have to see him before we take Doc Gilman out."

They parked on Main Street. They climbed the stairs to Mr. Norwood's law office over the drugstore.

Mr. Norwood was at his desk. He was a small man with a sharp, bony face.

"What can I do for you?" he asked.

Father told him about Dexter.

"What do you expect me to do?" asked Mr. Norwood.

"Nothing," said Father, "but we wanted to have a doctor look at the pony. Is it all right if we go into the timber?"

"I guess it's all right, this once," said the lawyer, "but that pony isn't mine, so don't be sending me any doctor bills."

"We didn't plan to send you any," said Father. He and Dave left without saying good-by.

They drove to Doc Gilman's house. The old doctor was sitting out in his yard. He listened carefully to what they had to say.

"I'll go out with you," he said.

They drove to the Arvin timber. They found the pony eating grass by the creek.

Doc Gilman went toward him. The pony shied away.

"Yes," said the doctor. "I see."

"I don't think his legs are broken," said Dave.

"No," said the doctor, "or he couldn't stand on them. It's the tendons in his hind legs—that's where the trouble is."

"Can you make him all right again?" asked Dave.

"I'm afraid not," said the doctor. "I'm afraid nobody can."

As they walked to the car, he and Father talked in low voices. Dave could not hear what they said.

They took the doctor back to town.

"I'll pay you for coming out," said Dave. "I don't have any money with me, but I have some in the bank."

"There's no charge," said the doctor.

Dave and Father thanked him. They started home.

"It surprises me," said Father, "that the pony could get out of the barn and into the timber. It surprises me that he can walk at all."

"He always was strong," said Dave, "and his legs weren't broken. I think he's going to get better."

"He won't get any better. Doc Gilman says there's no way to operate and tie the tendons back in place. If the pony belonged to me, I wouldn't want him to go on living that way."

"He doesn't belong to us," said Dave. "He belongs to Alex."

"But who knows were Alex is?" said Father.

"I'll hear from him," said Dave. "I'm sure to hear."

And the next day there was a letter from Alex. It was written in pencil on a page from a notebook:

Dear Dave,

   We are all right. I hope you are all right. We left Kansas City this morning and are on our way to St. Louis. You can write me there at the Blair Avenue Hotel.

                                                    Your friend
                                                    Alex

51

Rocker Horse

Dave tried to call Alex on the telephone. It was the first time he had ever called long-distance. A woman at the hotel told him, "There's no one here named Arvin."

"He must not be there yet," said Mother. "Why don't you write him a letter?"

Dave wrote to Alex:

It will be hard for you to believe this, but Dexter is alive. He was badly hurt, but he can now walk. Your Uncle Jon had a stroke and is in the hospital, so no one is left on the farm. I will look after Dexter until you come back. Let me know when you are coming. You can stay with me.

52

He asked Mother when his letter would get to St. Louis. "In about three days," she said.

"Alex will call me as soon as he gets it," said Dave.

But there was no call from Alex, and a week later Dave's letter came back. Beside Alex's name someone had written, "Not here."

He asked his mother, "What shall I do now?"

"Wait for him to write again," she said.

A month went by, with no letter from Alex.

Father saw Mr. Norwood in town one day and asked about Jon Arvin. "He's about the same," said the lawyer.

The "Keep Out" sign was still up at the Arvin place, but Dave went there almost every day.

"Why do you have to go there so much?" asked Father.

"I have to see if Dexter is all right," said Dave. He had made a feedbox and set it near the cabin. Sometimes he left salt in the box, or a few ears of corn. Almost always, when he went back, the salt had been licked up or the corn was gone.

Sometimes Dave found Dexter in the deepest, darkest part of the timber. He would talk to the pony as he knew Alex would have done. "Your mane and tail are full of burrs. I could comb them out if you'd stand still. Why won't you let me comb them out? You don't trust anyone, do you?"

Whenever he tried to go near Dexter, the pony shied away. He could not run, but he had learned to move quickly. He used his hind legs as a kind of crutch.

53

Now and then he came out into the pasture to eat grass. Dave and Wayne Ogle saw him there one day.

"There's old Rocker Horse," said Wayne.

Dave didn't answer.

"That's what I call him," said Wayne. "Old Rocker Horse."

"I heard you," said Dave.

"He's no good to himself or anyone else," said Wayne. "Somebody ought to shoot that old horse."

"You'd better not say that again," said Dave.

"Don't jump on me. I'm not the only one that says it."

"Who else says it?"

"My father, for one."

"That's what I thought."

"If you want to know the truth," said Wayne, "your father says it, too."

"I don't believe it," said Dave.

"Go ask him."

"I will."

Dave went home and told his Father what Wayne had said. "Did you say it?"

"All the neighbors have been talking about that pony," said Father. "None of us think it's right for him to go on suffering."

"But he's getting better. He can move better and faster than he could at first."

"He'll always be crippled."

"Does that mean he can't go on living?"

54

"He's all alone," said Father. "Nobody wants him. How long can he go on taking care of himself?"

"I'll take care of him," said Dave. "I'll bring him over here."

"You'll *not* bring him over here. I wouldn't have such an animal on my farm." Father sounded angry. "It's no kindness to the horse to let him go on like this. Can't you see that?"

"He's Alex's horse," said Dave. "We haven't any right to decide what to do with him."

"Alex is gone, and we may never see him again," said Father. "Somebody else may *have* to decide."

In the Timber

Summer ended and school began. It was Dave's last year in country school.

Mrs. Howard said, as she greeted the boys and girls, "You look different after summer vacation. You've all grown. Dave, you look the most different of all. You're so much taller."

He was older, too. He *felt* older.

More than once that fall the teacher said to him, "You aren't listening to me. Stop daydreaming!"

He wanted to tell her, I'm not daydreaming. I'm thinking.

Mostly he thought about people, and why they were the way they were. He thought how strange it was that someone

57

could be your best friend one day and gone from your life the next. He thought how many things could come between you and the plans you made.

One November morning Wayne Ogle caught up with him on the way to school. Wayne looked excited and important.

"I know something I'm not supposed to tell," he said.

Dave walked along without looking at him.

"Don't you want to know what it is?" asked Wayne.

"No," said Dave.

"I wasn't going to tell you anyway," said Wayne. But in the schoolyard, while they waited for the bell to ring, he said, "You won't be seeing old Rocker Horse anymore."

Dave was only half listening. "What?" he asked.

"I said, you won't be seeing that old pony anymore."

"Dexter? You mean Dexter? What are you talking about?"

Wayne laughed. "You're not going to find out any more from me."

The bell rang. Wayne started toward the schoolhouse. Dave caught him by the arm. "What about Dexter? Why won't I see him anymore?"

"That's for me to know and you to find out."

"*Tell* me!" Dave gave him a shove, and Wayne fell.

"Let me go." Wayne tried to get up. "The bell's ringing."

Dave sat on him, holding him down. "What about Dexter?"

"My father's going to shoot him, that's what!"

"You're lying," said Dave.

"I'm not."

58

"You *are* lying."

"No, I'm not. There was a meeting last night, and the men said—they said the pony couldn't live through the winter, and the thing to do was to shoot him—and my father is going to do it."

"When?" asked Dave.

"Now. This morning."

Dave jumped up. He began to run. Wayne shouted after him, "You'd better come back here! Didn't you hear the bell?"

Dave was already out of the schoolyard. He was running down the road toward Arvins' timber.

He climbed over the timber fence. He tried to think where the pony might be. In the oak grove? By the pool in the creek?

If he could drive him deeper into the timber where Mr. Ogle couldn't find him. . . .

He came to the creek. A man was there on the bank— Wayne's father in a red hunting jacket. He had a rifle in his hands.

On the other side of the creek was Dexter, his head up, his eyes watching.

"Don't!" cried Dave.

Mr. Ogle almost dropped the rifle. "What are *you* doing here?"

"Don't do it," said Dave. "You *can't* do it!"

"Don't tell me what I can't do." Mr. Ogle lifted the rifle.

Dexter was still watching. He seemed to be waiting.

Mr. Ogle took aim. He stopped and rubbed his eyes. He said to Dave, "Go somewhere else. Go on—get out!"

He aimed again. He took a step forward, almost as if he wanted to frighten the pony away. But Dexter stood quietly.

Mr. Ogle was shaking. He said, "Why does he have to keep looking at me? I can't do it when he looks at me—when you both look at me!"

He put the rifle over his shoulder and went stamping away. Dave heard his steps in the dry leaves. Then the timber was still.

Dave felt weak. There was a blur in front of his eyes. When he could see again, he looked across the creek. Dexter was gone.

End of Waiting

Afterward Dave heard his father and mother talking about Mr. Ogle.

"He said he could do it," said Father. "He wasn't as brave as he thought he was."

"Maybe you wouldn't be so brave if you tried it," said Mother. "It looks as if none of the other men are going to be so brave, either."

And Father didn't answer.

Wayne Ogle said at school, "That old horse won't get through the winter anyway."

Before the start of cold weather, Dave went to the timber and built a shed against the cabin. He made it of poles and covered the roof with dry grass so the pony would have shelter.

When the creek froze, Dave chopped holes in the ice so Dexter could have water.

Dave took corn to the timber, although Dexter had learned to find his own food. Under the ice and snow were dry leaves and grass with seeds and acorns among them.

One day in January Dave found the pony standing in a hollow near the creek. He went nearer. Dexter shook his mane and rolled his eyes, without moving from where he stood.

Dave spoke to him. "Aren't you going to run away? After all this time, are you going to trust me?"

Then he saw what had happened. The pony's feet were sunk in the mud. He was trapped there.

With a piece of tree root, Dave tried to dig him free. The mud was stiff and half frozen. The piece of root broke in his hands.

He said to Dexter, "Don't worry. I'll get you out."

He found a flat rock that was sharp on one side. With the rock he began to dig the mud away from the pony's hoofs.

"Now," he said. "Two good steps and you're out." He gave the pony a little slap on the side. Dexter threw himself forward. He dragged himself out of the mud. His sides and legs were trembling.

"Whoa," said Dave. "Let me scrape you off."

But Dexter went lunging away.

After that day it seemed to Dave that the pony was never

quite the same again. He was more shy than ever. He moved more slowly.

Night after night Dave woke and thought of Dexter alone in the timber. He thought of what Wayne Ogle had said— "That old horse won't get through the winter."

But on the first warm day of spring, Dexter came hobbling out into the pasture. He was so thin that every rib showed. His eyes were dull and tired. And Dave saw that the pony had grown old.

Spring passed, and most of summer. One afternoon, while Dave was trimming the hedge along the road, a car came by. A young man jumped out. The car went on.

The young man was tall and brown. He wore a hat that shaded his face. "Dave—?" he said.

"Yes." Dave put down his ax.

"You don't know me." The young man came closer.

Dave stood still. "Alex!" he said.

They shook hands.

"Are you all right?" asked Alex.

"Yes," said Dave. "Are you?"

"Yes." Alex began rather quickly, "I've been all over since I saw you last. We went back to the circus. Then we had a chance to work on this ranch in Texas, and that's where we are now." He was looking up and down the road. "It looks the same. I didn't know whether it would or not. I didn't even know if you'd remember me."

"I remember you," said Dave.

"You didn't answer my letter," said Alex, "but I know how it is. You get busy with things—"

"I answered it," said Dave.

"You did?"

"My letter came back. It's funny, I still remember the name of that hotel in St. Louis. The Blair Avenue Hotel."

"We were there," said Alex. "But maybe when your letter came, we hadn't got there yet. It took us a while to get from Kansas City to St. Louis."

"In that letter I wrote you about your Uncle Jon—"

"I know about him," said Alex.

"You do?"

"Yes. After what he did, we thought we never wanted to see him again. But then my father said we shouldn't blame him too much, because he was sick. He wrote to him last week. The letter went to his lawyer, and the lawyer wrote to us. My father and I came up. He's at the hospital now. I hitchhiked out here, and my father is going to pick me up. But don't let me keep you from your work. I'll just wait around—"

"Do you know about—about Dexter?" asked Dave.

"If you don't mind," said Alex, "I'd rather not talk about it."

"All right. I just wanted to know if you'd seen him."

"*Seen* him?"

"Dexter is alive," said Dave.

Alex turned pale.

Dave told him what had happened.

Alex asked, almost in a whisper, "Where is he?"

"On your old place," said Dave. "Do you want to go over there?"

They walked to the Arvin place and into the timber. They passed the cabin with the shed on one side of it.

"You made that for him, didn't you?" said Alex. "You put that feedbox there."

They went on.

"Are you *sure* he's here?" asked Alex.

"I saw him two days ago," said Dave, and he began to feel afraid.

They came to the far side of the timber. Alex had been walking ahead. He stopped. There among the trees was Dexter. He started away, his hind legs dragging through the grass. He looked back at them through the matted hair that hung over his eyes.

"He knows me," said Alex. "Dexter—"

He began to cry.

Later, as Dave and Alex walked back through the timber, Dave asked, "Can you stay with us tonight?"

"No. My father said he'd stop for me. But he'll bring me back tomorrow."

In the morning Alex and his father were back, in a pickup truck with "Sunny Acres Ranch" painted on the door. Hitched to the truck was a horse trailer.

Dave rode with them to the old Arvin place. He went with them into the timber. They found the pony not far from where he had been the day before.

Alex had brought a halter and rope. He slipped the halter over Dexter's head.

"Come on," he said. "I'm taking you home. You and I are going to Texas. Now what do you think of that?" And Dexter let himself be led through the timber and across the pasture.

Dave opened the gate. The three of them half lifted, half pushed the pony into the trailer.

Alex's father said to Dave, "Get in. We'll take you back to your house."

"No, thank you," said Dave. "It's hard to turn around with the trailer. I'll walk."

"Good-by," said Alex. "I'll see you."

"I'll see you," said Dave.

The truck and the trailer pulled away. They were out of sight.

Dave looked down the empty road. Alex was gone again. Now Dexter was gone, too. Yet they would never really be gone, because of the way he remembered them.

Alex on the trapezes.

Alex racing along on the pony.

Dexter coming out of the timber in the spring.

Now he could imagine a new picture. Dexter in a green pasture with a barn nearby, and the house where Alex lived. Alex talking to the pony, and the pony listening.

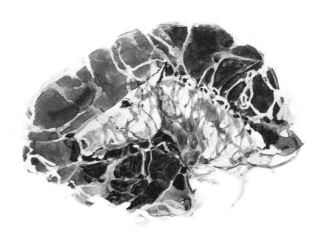

About the Author

Clyde Robert Bulla is one of America's best-known writers for young people today. The broad scope of his interests has led him to write more than forty fine books on a variety of subjects, including travel, history, science, and music. He has been widely praised for his rare ability to write simply yet with great warmth and sensitivity. Mr. Bulla was given the Silver Medal of the Commonwealth Club of California for his distinguished contribution to the field of children's books, and in 1972 his book *Pocahontas and the Strangers* received the Christopher Award.

Clyde Bulla's early years were spent on a farm near King City, Missouri, and only after the chores were done could he devote himself to reading and writing. He now lives and works in the bustling city of Los Angeles. When he is not busy writing a book, he loves to travel.

About the Artist

Glo Coalson grew up in Abilene, Texas, and was educated at Abilene Christian College, the University of Colorado, and the University of Texas. She now lives in New York City, with her dog, Meat Loaf, but spends several months a year with her family in Texas. Her occupation is art—graphics, drawing, painting, sculpture, and ceramics. She says that there seems to be no distinction between her vocation and her hobbies, except that she also enjoys fishing, camping, and folk music.